S is for San Francisco
Copyright © 2017 by Dry Climate Inc.

Printed in the United States

First edition

www.dryclimatestudios.com

ISBN
978-1-9424023-4-3

Library of Congress Control Number
2017900778

S is for San Francisco

Written by Maria Kernahan
Illustrated by Michael Schafbuch

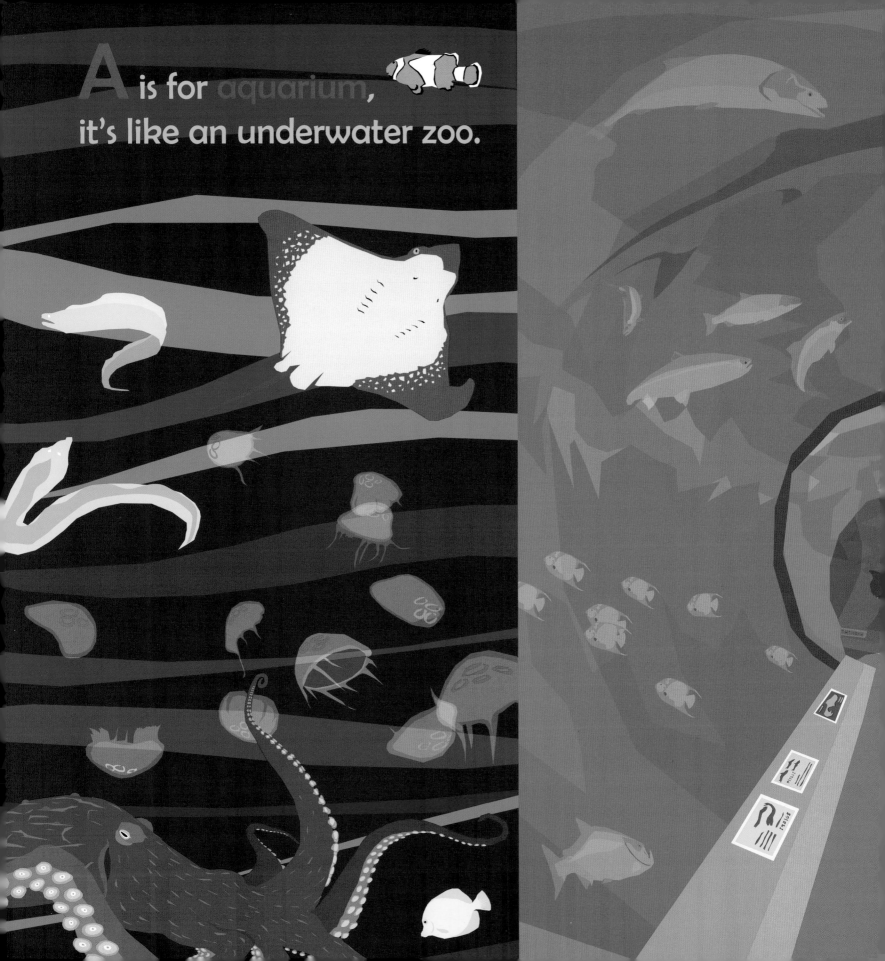

A is for aquarium,
it's like an underwater zoo.

One is not enough,
in San Francisco we have two!

B is for the **blanket** of fog the creeps across the Bay.

It happens when hot inland air meets the ocean's spray.

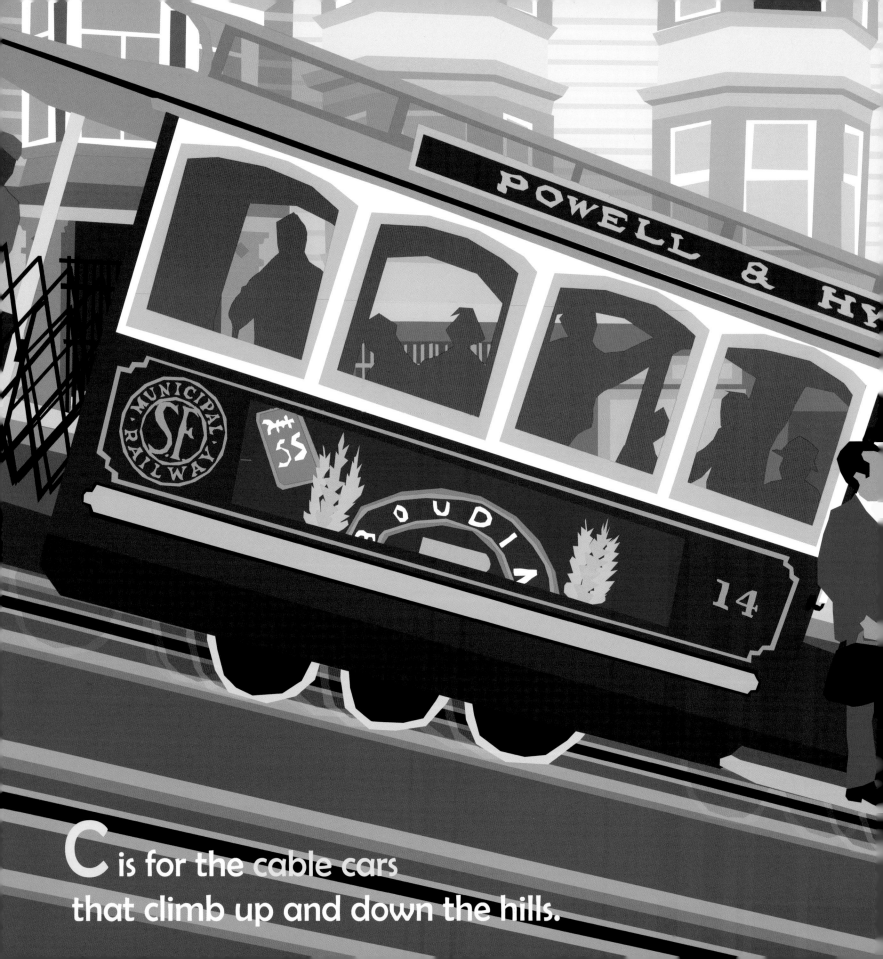

C is for the cable cars
that climb up and down the hills.

Hang on tight when you hop on,
the ride is such a thrill!

D is for the Dungeness crabs
that live deep down in the brine.

They're caught in wire crab pots
and pulled in on a line.

E is for The Embarcadero,
catch a ride out on the dock.

You'll find the famous Ferry Building
underneath the clock.

F is for fortune cookies, they are a Chinatown treat.

Crack one open and you may find a forecast that is sweet.

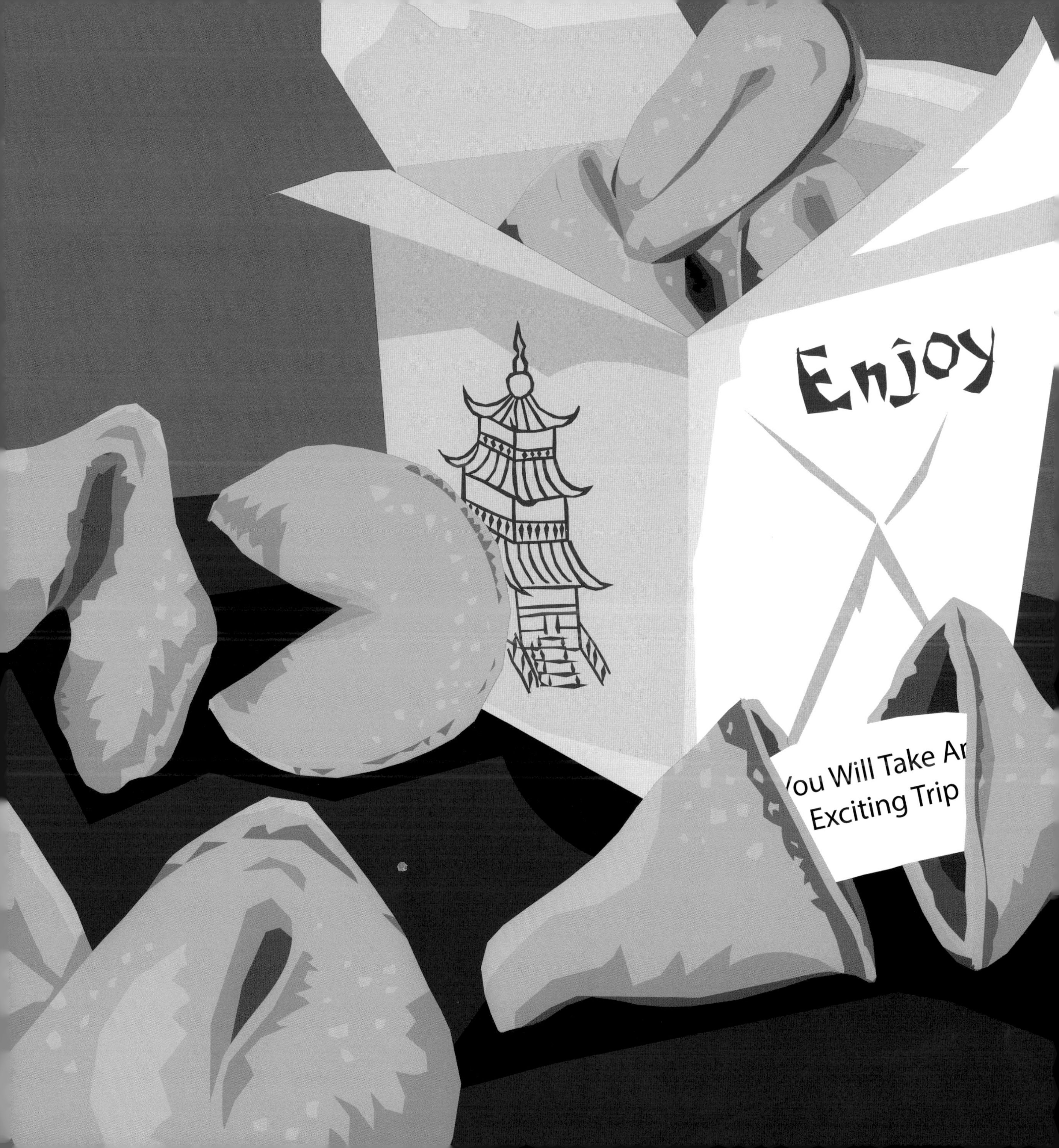
Enjoy
You Will Take An
Exciting Trip

G is for Golden Gate Park,
it's San Francisco's own backyard.

There are so many things to do,
picking one is just so hard!

H is for the splash hits
that land out in the bay.

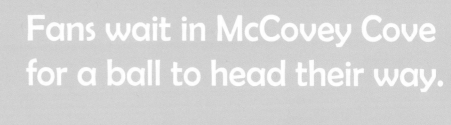

Fans wait in McCovey Cove
for a ball to head their way.

I is for Italian Ice and gelato in North Beach.

Can't decide between the two?
Then have a scoop of each!

J is for jerseys of our favorite teams.

Each season we start fresh with championship dreams.

K is for the kites that are flown with expertise.

At Crissy Field it's easy with a gusty bayside breeze.

L is for lighthouse that stands on Alcatraz isle.
The beacon shines out on the bay,
you can see the light for miles.

M is for the medallions
you'll find down at your feet.

They mark a trail of history through San Francisco's streets.

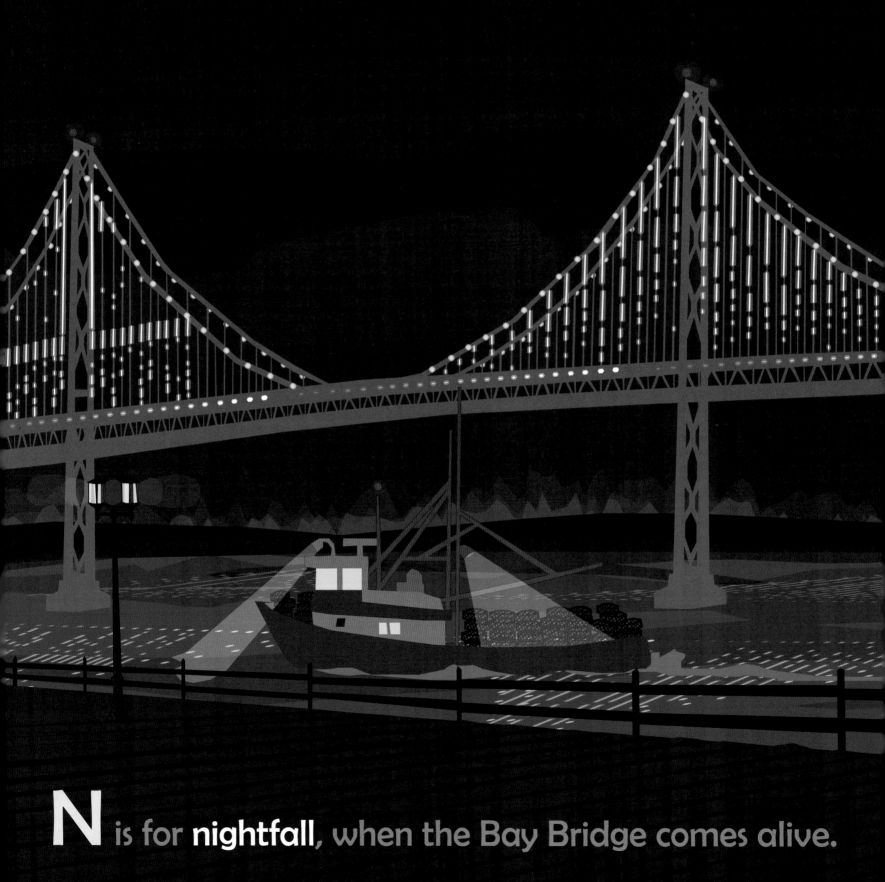

N is for **nightfall**, when the Bay Bridge comes alive.

Dazzling lights illuminate the water and the sky.

O is for the **"oohs"** and "aahs" heard throughout the halls.

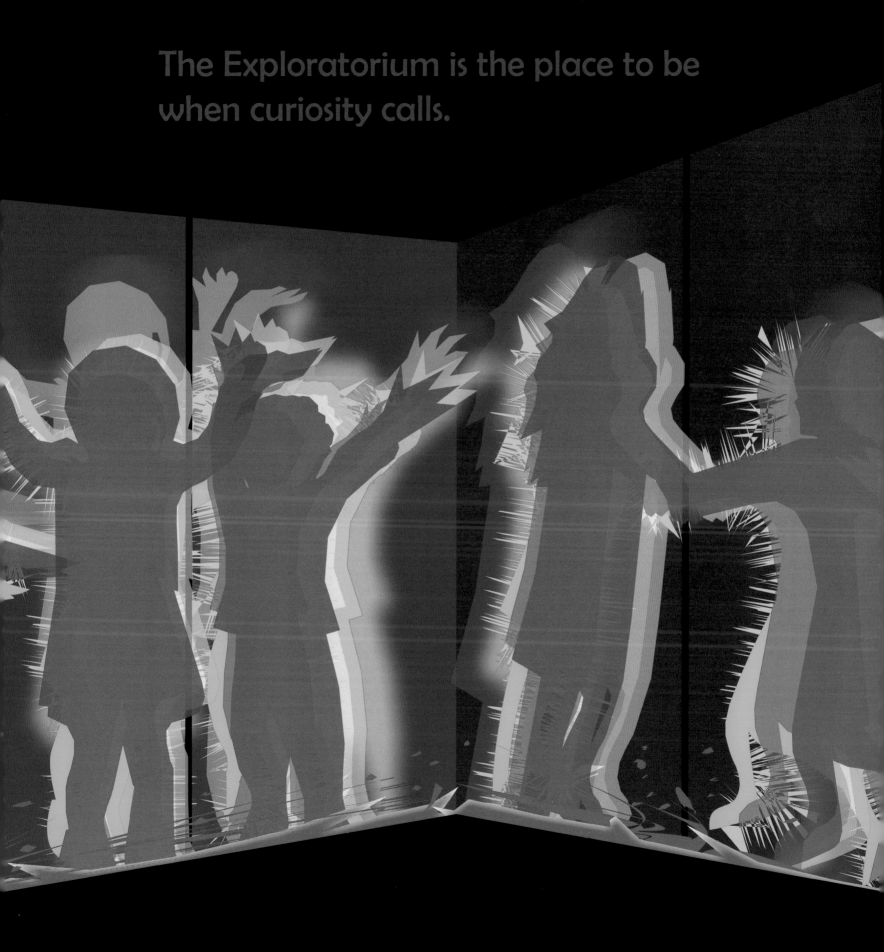

The Exploratorium is the place to be when curiosity calls.

P is for the parrots
found on Telegraph Hill.

Can you spot them all?
You can hear them chirp and trill.

Q is for **quake**, it makes buildings shift and sway.

The big one happened long ago,
perhaps a little one today?

R is for the roar of the sea lions at the pier.

When you hear their yips and barks
you'll know that you are near.

S is for San Francisco, the city by the bay.
49 square miles that will take your breath away.

T is for the Tea Garden
that was built for the World's Fair.

It's the perfect place to go
for peace and some fresh air.

U is for Union Square,
where in winter you can skate.

Take a spin around the rink,
can you carve a figure eight?

V is for the **views**
from Mission Dolores Park.

Spread out a picnic blanket
and stay until it's dark.

W is for humpback whales -
they are noted for their ridge.

Sometimes you can spot them
swimming underneath the bridge.

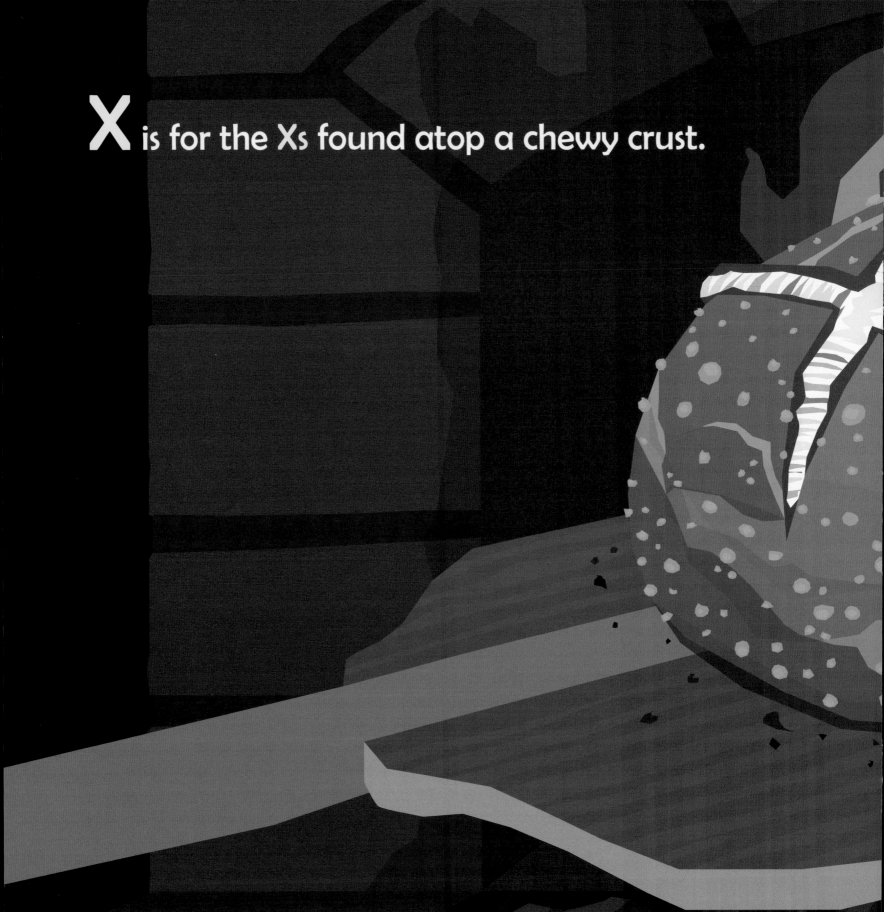

X is for the Xs found atop a chewy crust.

San Francisco sourdough is a culinary must.

Y is for yellow, next to green and red and blue.

The pretty "Painted Ladies" come in every hue.

Z is for the **zig-zag** of hilly Lombard Street.
Driving down is easy, walking up is quite a feat!

T is for Thank you, it's not just a letter.
Your help was amazing, it made us much better.

Christopher and Matthew, Meggie, Claire and Libby,
Maureen and Big Daddy.

Thanks to the folks who helped us along the way.
We need the extra eyes, big and little!

The Gales
The Greggs
The Judsons
The Levy-Howards
The McAdams
The Other Judsons
Joe Schafbuch
Tim Schafbuch
Ali Williams

A portion of the proceeds from this book
will be donated to literacy programs in
San Francisco through DonorsChoose.org.

OTHER BOOKS IN THE ALPHABET SERIES FROM DRY CLIMATE STUDIOS:

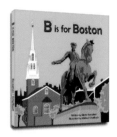

FOR PRINTS, BOOKS AND GIFTS PLEASE VISIT
www.dryclimatestudios.com